The Gynecologist

Hot Erotic Short Stories Illustrated with Hentai Pictures

Emily White

TABLE OF CONTENTS

TABLE OF CONTENTS_____5

INTRODUCTION_____7

THE GYNECOLOGIST _____9

CHAPTER 1 _____10

CHAPTER 2 _____19

CHAPTER 3 _____30

CHAPTER 4 _____37

RECREATIONAL AFTERNOONS _____49

CHAPTER 1 _____50

CHAPTER 2 _____61

CHAPTER 3 _____70

CHAPTER 4 _____77

CHAPTER 5 _____83

INTRODUCTION

Welcome to a captivating journey where my enthralling stories seamlessly intertwine with enchanting illustrations that redefine the very essence of desire in the world of hentai erotica.

Within the secret pages of these forbidden tales, I invite you to immerse yourself in a fiery universe of unrestrained passion. Every word is a whispered moan, and each illustration is a visual embrace that transforms the realms of fantasy into tangible reality.

This collection is not for the faint of heart. It's a bold manifesto, an invitation urging you to delve into the dark depths of lust, where pleasure is painted with audacious strokes and details that promise to quicken the rhythm of your heart. The illustrations are provocative gateways, guiding you into sensual dimensions where every hidden desire finds its expression without remorse.

Are you ready to plunge into a whirlwind of seduction and temptation, where the pages themselves transform into a stage for your most secret fantasies? Allow yourself to be carried away into a realm where sin transforms into art, and art seamlessly merges harmoniously with the ecstasy of desire.

Lift the cover and prepare for an experience ignited by the flame of passion. This is not just another collection; it's your exclusive ticket to the boldest manifestations of anime eros, written masterfully by me, **Emily White**.

THE GYNECOLOGIST

CHAPTER 1

Eleonora folds the piece of paper in her pocket. She does not dare to read it. And yet! Fifteen days late! This had never happened to her before. Her period had always come on the day it was supposed to. She left her older friends at school without even kissing Maria and walked aimlessly down the sidewalk.

Fifteen days late! Nothing since they both returned from their ski vacations. She didn't even mention it to her cousin, with whom she spent that week supposedly skiing. Well, they skied, but not only that!

She has a decision to make. She has in her pocket, written on the piece of paper she is shuffling, the details of a Doctor Luc recommended.

Luc.

She sees again the young instructor and his friend Marc, with whom Maria and they shared every night in the chalet. No wonder she is late! Being a virgin before this vacation, she hadn't thought to protect herself.

How unconscionable! And even if it had only been the two young men! The red of shame rises in her face as she remembers the torrid last night in the office of Bernard the manager in the company of Maria, the two monitors, Lucille the monitor, the cook and his assistant. Fucking, sucking, fucking, it was all there! Several times! And to think that before this stay she dreamed of arriving at the wedding as a virgin and indulging her Prince Charming on her wedding night!

Eleonora sits on a bench. It's a disaster if she's pregnant! How will she dare pass the baccalaureate with a protruding belly? And what will her mother say? No, it's impossible, she can't, she doesn't want to have a baby.... Not right away... Not until she's married.... And she has time for that, having just come of age. Her last hope is there, in her pocket. Luc has assured her that Jean-Paul is very understanding and will know what to do if there is a problem. And now she has a problem, and a big one! But is it the kind of problem this Jean-Paul can handle?

She doesn't dare pull the paper out of his pocket. She's been carrying it around for a week, putting off opening it and reading the phone number. She can't procrastinate any longer. Earlier, in chemistry, she was nauseous. Everyone in the class, including the teacher, thought it was because of the unpleasant smell of the experiment going on, but she doubts it. Gathering her courage, she pulls out the piece of paper and opens it. A name, the address of a hospital where this Jean-Paul has his practice, and a phone number.

Five o'clock in the afternoon. The doctor must be in his office. He opens his cell phone and dials the number.

- Hello!

- This is Dr. Jean-Paul Méjean speaking. I am listening.

- I am calling on behalf of Luc Méjean. He told me that if I had any problems, I should come to you.

- Did he do that? When did he tell you?

- Two weeks ago. I was on a skiing vacation where he is an instructor.

- I see. Who am I talking to?

- My name is Eleonora Girard, I'm a senior at the high school of...

- You don't have to give me that information, Miss Eleonora. Do you want a date?

- Um... I think so.

- Give me a number where I can call you back. I'll have to check my schedule, which I don't have available.

- You can reach me at 06...

- I have it. I'll call you back in about an hour. Goodbye Miss.

The doctor hangs up. Eleonora looked at her mute cell phone. An hour of waiting! She won't come home until she knows....

Jean-Paul consults his address book.

- Luc... Luc... Ah, here's the number for the chalet. What time is it? Five past ten? They must all be back by now.

He dials the number.

- Hello!... Hello sir... May I speak to Mr. Luc Méjean?... Yes, I will hold.

Jean-Paul opens the diary he said he did not have.

- If what you think is true, I'll be able to call you Thursday evening at seven, when Josette has gone out... Hello, is that you, Luc? This is Jean Paul.

- Good evening Jean-Paul, to what do I owe the pleasure of having you on the line?

- Well, it's a pleasure to greet you, my dear nephew, how are these ski trips going? I just had a curious phone call from a certain Eleonora Girard who.... Well, to tell you the truth, I don't know. She wants to see me, do you have any idea?

- Uh... I suspected that, that's why I gave her your address.

- Tell me about it. Did you have a good time together?

- Very, very, very good times.

- No kidding!

- Since she was a virgin at the beginning of the trip....

- Which she isn't anymore, is she?

- Uh... You know me, uncle.

- I don't like it when you call me uncle. What did you mean by that?

- I was saying, since she was a virgin, I don't think she's on the pill and since we didn't take any precautions....

- You don't have to draw me a picture, your girlfriend is pregnant!

- Probably.

- And since you're not a fatherly person....

- Um, I wasn't alone.

- All the more reason to pass it on, is that what you're asking?

- Well...

- Well, I'll call your protégé and see what needs to be done.

- Keep me informed. I'll leave you, I'm needed for animations. Goodbye... uncle.

Luc hangs up before hearing Jean-Paul's reproaches. He stretches out in his armchair. Knowing his nephew's taste, he thinks that at the moment the young virgin must be in the know! Why not try to take advantage of it? Later he calls this line and makes an appointment with her at a discreet time. He presses the intercom button.

- Josette please bring in the next patient....

Eleonora consults her watch for the umpteenth time. Quarter to six. What is this doctor waiting for to call her back? Ten times he's picked up her cell phone, ten times he's put it back in her purse. What will he think of her if she calls him again? Ah, the ringtone.

- No, I can't talk to you right now, Maria, I'm waiting for an important call...yes...I'll call you back...see you later.

She disconnects the call. A few seconds later, the phone rings again.

- Hello, Miss Eleonora Girard?

Uff, the doctor!

- Yes, it's me.

- This is Dr. Jean-Paul Méjean. I'll call you back as promised. Could you come to my office at Hospital X.... let's say Thursday at the end of the afternoon? I will bring you after my consultations.

- The day after tomorrow? Okay, doctor...

- I'll be expecting you at seven o'clock in the evening. Ask for the gynecology department, room 303, in the lobby.

- Room 303, got it.

- All right, see you Thursday, miss.

Eleonora folds her cell phone. She feels better, she is no longer alone. On the way home, she thought of her cousin, of the tender caresses exchanged in their bed when Luc and Marc left them in the morning. Since their return, despite Maria's efforts, they have not had the opportunity to isolate themselves. This is probably the reason for the phone call earlier. Does she want it? She can't say.

She has the impression that until she is sure, it will be impossible for her to enjoy herself.

She opens the door with her key.

- Is that you, honey?" asks her mother from the kitchen.

- Yes, Mom.

- Guess who's coming to visit!

- I don't know, Mom... Oh, it's you!" she exclaimed when she saw Maria enter the hallway.

- Yes, it's me! You don't seem to like it.

- Yes, yes, come into my room.

Madame Girard is about to go out.

- I'll leave you girls, I must go out. Eleonora, don't wait for me to go to bed, I'll be back late. There's some leftover roast in the refrigerator. There's enough for both of us if you want to stay, Maria.

- Thank you, Aunt.

- Well, I'll leave you to it, be good.

Beatrice Girard kisses her daughter and niece.

- You took a long time to come from school! I've been waiting for an hour, what did you do?

- Um, an errand.

She doesn't want to talk to Maria about her fears, not yet. She hugs her cousin and tries to kiss her. Eleonora turns her head and then, unable to bear it any longer, puts her lips on his half-open mouth. How sweet that tongue is! Why has she been deprived of it for two weeks?

- Aah!

- You know," Maria admits, "I thought you were mad at me.

- Why would I be angry with you? What would I be angry about?

- Well, at the cottage...um.... it was kind of my fault... um... You were a virgin.

- No, don't worry, I don't regret anything that happened to us there. I don't.

- Not even our caresses? You didn't want to, I had to force you.

- I can't remember!

The line takes Maria's mouth. Embraced, they reach the girl's room and fall on the bed. A battle follows, clothes fly off, they stop only in bra and panties, not daring to continue.

- I have to take a shower," says Eleonora.

- I'll come with you.

Squeezed together in the small cabin, the two girls rub each other. A long kiss, hands go down to the belly, fingers creep into the slit and search for the opposite vulva. Suddenly Eleonora pulls away.

- Let's get out!

Maria, disappointed, follows her. Eleonora wraps herself in a bath sheet and refuses her cousin's help.

- What is your problem? Don't you love me anymore?

- Oh yes, but...

Eleonora is tired of keeping a secret that is too heavy for her. She bursts into tears on her cousin's shoulder.

- There, there... calm down... Did someone hurt you?

- I... think... I... I...

- You... Are you pregnant?

- I... think so.

- You're not on the pill?

- No... no.

- Sorry love, it's my fault, I should have warned you.

- Warned me about what? You know, when I left for my ski vacation, I had no idea that I was going to.... uh...

- That you were going to lose your virginity," Maria completed in the face of her cousin's hesitation. Have you had a consultation?

- 'No, not yet, I... I have an appointment for the day after tomorrow.

- Then it's not safe. You could be wrong.

- Do you think so?" asks Eleonora, ready to grab any hope.

Maria cuddles her cousin.

- You say, what will you do if it's true?

- I...I don't know.

Suddenly she bursts into tears again.

- I... I don't want... I don't want to have a child!

- That's it...that's it...you don't have to worry in advance.

Eleonora feverishly searches her cousin's mouth. She desperately needs a caress. The two girls lie down on the bed....

CHAPTER 2

Eleonora looks at her watch. Ten to seven. We have to go! She procrastinated for almost fifteen minutes. The security guard at the entrance first stared at her with curiosity, then, since the girl had no intention of entering, lost interest, mistaking her for someone waiting for an exit. Eleonora took advantage of the guard's momentary absence to sneak inside.

There are few people in the room at this time of day when the consultations are over. No one pays attention to the girl. Glancing at the map in the lobby, the gynecology service is on the third floor.

- Room 303, that's normal, she murmurs.

She climbs the stairs, not wanting to draw attention from the noise of the elevator. A plaque on door 303 reads Doctor J.P. Méjean. The line hesitates. A heavy sigh, then he knocks.

- Enter.

- Are you Doctor Méjean?

- Yes, and this is Miss Eleonora Girard.... Come in, Miss.

The line enters the vast office. In one corner, a consultation bed covered with a large white paper and devices with screens larger than a television set. The doctor is sitting at his desk by the window.

- Please close the door and sit down.

At that moment you hear the bells of the hospital chapel ring seven times.

- You are just in time, this is very good, thank you.

Eleanor sits down in the chair reserved for patients. Jean-Paul gives her an engaging smile. He is not a bad doctor, he looks like Luc,

20

only older," he says. She thinks her nephew has good taste: ("She's a pretty girl, I can't wait to see her naked.").

- So you know Luc, my nephew.

("Ah, that's the reason for the resemblance"). Eleonora squirms in her chair.

- Yes, he was an instructor at the chalet where I spent a week's ski vacation.

- Ah, very good, very good. Why don't you tell me why you want to see me?

After some hesitation, Eleonora confided in the doctor. She tells him her concern about the unusual delay in her menstruation. She admits to having sex with Luc and others.

- Didn't you think to protect yourself?

- Um, no. I... was a virgin.

- That's no reason! What do they teach you in school in sex education?

Eleonora bows her head. Yes, she has to admit, what was the point of knowing everything about procreation and contraceptives?

- Well, that's the past. Let's not keep talking about it, it's pointless. Take off your clothes so I can examine you.

- In... everything?

- Sure, sure.

She puts her things on the back of the chair. In bra and panties she hesitates.

- Completely!

Eleonora bites her lip but obeys. First she takes off her bra, then her panties. Jean-Paul swallows her saliva. She's a piece of work, this girl! A real beauty, not like those anorexic girls who want to look like starving models.

- Lie down on the exam table.... Yes, put your feet in those stirrups.... Yes... Like this.

Strangely, being immodestly spread out excites her instead of filling her with shame as she expected. Jean-Paul approaches her looking very professional. He caresses her breasts. Immediately the nipples rise.

- Your breasts are sensitive, aren't they?

- Yes, yes, yes," stutters the young girl, who is trembling from the contact.

- It's a sign, you're probably pregnant.

- Oh no!

Jean-Paul caresses the tender globes. He has always loved to feel the breasts of his young clients and she lets him, pressing her lips together to stifle her sighs. After several minutes, he leaves her breasts, much to Eleonora's displeasure, to take a barbaric instrument in his hand.

- I will examine you more thoroughly.

He positions himself between her open legs. Eleonora's eyes go wide. The device seems enormous to her. What a diameter! It can't fit! It's bigger than... Luc's tail looms before her eyes... and Louis is even bigger, but less voluminous in his memory than this device that Jean-Paul wants to examine him with.

- Are you... are you going to... stick it in me?

- Yes, it is necessary.

- Does it... does it hurt?

- Yes, if you don't relax.

- I... I don't want to.

- You have to.

He pretends to present the huge instrument.

- I'm...I'm scared, doctor.

- There may be a way... suggests Jean-Paul as he withdraws the device.

- Say doctor.

- The introduction would be easier if you could prepare yourself with a... um... with a vaginal massage.

- Oh yes, please! Please," Eleonora begs, ready to do anything to avoid the pain.

Jean-Paul puts down the dreaded device and puts on a pair of surgical gloves. He wants to give, at least at first, a serious look to an undertaking that is not at all serious. He pushes down on his middle finger. The line groans.

- Relax... There... Yes... Let go, he advises as the dew of pleasure appears. The better you accept the intrusion, the easier the examination will be.

He withdraws the glove and dips his finger again, quickly joined by another.

- Aah! sighs Eleonora.

- Yes, that's good," she encourages as she pushes her fingers in and out while rubbing her clit with her thumb.

- Aah!... Aaah!

In her mind she is no longer on the exam table but on the couch in the office of Bernard, the manager of the apartment, getting fucked. In a flash of clarity, she realizes that the doctor, under the guise of an exam, is about to abuse her... No, don't abuse, accept, she desires from the depths of her being to feel penetrated. Pressing into the stirrups, she meets the phalanges that pierce her.

Jean-Paul judges her ready for the next scene. He withdraws his fingers, heaving a reproachful sigh, and opens his intimate lips to examine the vaginal orifice from which a rivulet of powder is pouring.

- 'I'm afraid it's not enough,' she says.

- What-what should we do?

- Maybe continue the massage with a natural... er... device.

- Like the one you have between your legs?" replied Eleonora, showing that she was not fooled by the doctor's maneuvers.

- For example," smiled Jean-Paul, pulling out her bandaged sex from under her gown.

The girl shuddered.

- 'I... I think the massage will be effective with this,' Eleanor murmured, her eyes fixed on the shaft as it advanced, taking position between her open thighs... Aaah! Yes!... massage me!... Yes!...harder!

He grabs Jean-Paul by the hips and accompanies his loins. He regrets that his feet are trapped in the stirrups and he can't grip his slayer with his thighs.

- Han!... The... Han!... massage... Han!... must be complete to... Han!... to be effective, she gasps.

- Yes... Aaaah!... Complete... Aaaah!... Mmmh!... Yes!... Ouii!... Ouiii!

Jean-Paul tries to gag the girl to muffle her screams. It's useless. Fortunately there is no one in the ward at this hour. He is no longer the one leading the fight. The line is wild. Luc was right when he told her that this girl was a real catch!

The door opens slowly, a tall black man in a white coat with a bright smile closes behind him.

- Ah!...you're... Han!...you're here Désiré.... Han!" stammers Jean-Paul.

- Yes, I came to see if you need help, you're making such a racket!

- No-no!... Han!... Yes!" he snaps back, to.... Han!... wait... Han!...a little bit of you.... Han!... you will take control.

Eleonora, in the middle of her waxing, doesn't hear the dialogue and continues to moan louder. Désiré removes his underpants and panties from under his blouse and begins polishing a very large sex to make it hard.

The contractions of Eleonora's vagina overcome the doctor's resistance and he bursts out moaning.

- Aaaah!... Aaaah!... Arrrghh!... Aaaahhh!

He breathes for a good minute before withdrawing. Eleanor continues to shake her head from side to side. Her casual lover has

25

jilted her, she doesn't know how to reconnect with the fun that is running away from her.

- Line, my dear, we are in luck. We have at our disposal a natural massage tool even more effective than mine... look," she adds, showing off her huge shaft.

- Ooh!

- I think the massage will be even better with this device.

- Oh yes!... Better...

The desire positions itself, the monstrous glans makes its way inside, dilating the flesh.

- Aaah!... Yes!... I feel the massage... Aaarrrggghh!

The orgasm erupts without warning. Eleonora turns her head in all directions. Jean-Paul caresses her forehead and breasts while Désiré pushes in and out at a steady pace...

Everything has an end... After a phase of acceleration, Désiré collapses in an incomprehensible gurgle. Eleonora, shaken by several successive orgasms, slowly recovers. Jean-Paul removes his colleague and presents a smaller speculum of the torture instrument Eleonora was so afraid of. He pushes it in effortlessly.

- That's it! The massage has been effective, we can perform the examination.

With a pump he frees the vagina from the sperm clogging it.

- Hiii! It tickles!

The doctor continues the exploration.

- Well... Yes ... so ... so ... Line, lift the pelvis... yes... like that, you can put it down.... You can get dressed now.

Eleonora staggers to her feet. Désiré picks her up and leads her to the armchair where she rests for a while before putting on her underwear.

- Well, since you don't need me anymore, I'll leave you to it," says the black doctor as he pulls up his underwear.

- No, please stay, I haven't finished.

Désiré puts his jeans back on and sits down next to Eleonora.

- Well, I can confirm that you are pregnant, young lady, by about three weeks.

- Ooh, so it was true. What...what am I about to...? become?

- You don't want to hold it, I'll take it.

- Oh, no! Never!

- So you're volunteering for an abortion?

- Will my mother know?

- You are of age, not us or the hospital administration.

Eleonora calms down and wipes away her tears. She is still almost naked, having put on only her underwear. Jean-Paul and Désiré smile at the spectacle.

- When can I come? Are you the one who will be practicing?

- If you don't mind, with the help of Désiré here, our best anesthesiologist.

- Oh, is that so? Are you also a doctor?

- At your service, miss," smiled the tall black man, bowing.

- 'Even if this little operation is benign, I would prefer to keep you under surveillance for a whole night,' Jean-Paul continued.

- An entire night? What am I going to tell my mother?

- I don't know, pretend to sleep at a friend's house for example.

Jean-Paul consults his diary.

- It's Thursday... Are you free the day after tomorrow?

- Saturday? Um...

- Please... yes? Well, show up, Miss Eleonora, Saturday night at seven like today.

- Already? Can't it wait?

- The sooner it ends, the less you'll have to suffer. You have to strike while the iron's hot.

- Does it hurt?

- You don't feel...

Jean-Paul interrupts Désiré.

- It depends... Yes, in some cases.

-Ah!...um... you... you're going to prepare me like tonight, aren't you?

The two doctors smiled. They had intended to do it, and the fact that it was the girl who had suggested it removed any qualms. Eleonora sighed and began to get dressed.

- Wait a minute," says Désiré, leaving the office.

He returns with a small briefcase.

- I'll take some blood.

- I'll take some blood.

- It is essential, Miss Eleonora.

Eleonora grimaces as the needle goes in, more out of apprehension than pain. The anesthesiologist questions the girl and fills out a questionnaire.

- Well, I think everything is in order," he says as he puts the suitcase away, "See you Saturday night.

- See you on Saturday night.

- Oh, I forgot, don't eat.

- Shouldn't I eat?

- Or drink," Jean-Paul says, starting at noon. This avoids the post-op problems caused by anesthesia.

He gets up, looks around the hallway, there is no one there.

- Eleonora, I'm not taking you home, it's safer for you to go out alone. I'll see you at seven o'clock on Saturday in this office.

She closes behind her.

The hospital is dark, only the security lights faintly illuminate the corridor. The young girl, still in shock, finds her way out. The attendant gives her only a distracted glance. He is there to guard the nighttime entrances, not the exits. At nine o'clock in the evening, Eleonora sighs. She will have to invent an excuse to justify

her lateness and prepare her mother for her absence on Saturday
night....

CHAPTER 3

The line shows up at the appointed time. Twenty times during the day and the previous one, racked with remorse, she almost phoned to say she was giving up, twenty times she put down the receiver, terrified at the thought of bringing a child into the world barely out of infancy. No, she made the right decision, the only one possible in her case.

Yes, she will want children, yes, she will be happy to be a mother, but not right away, not until she has tasted life! She has the feeling of having walked through a door of no return when she finds herself in the hospital lobby.

There is no crowd, even less than two days before. Like the day before, she slowly climbs the stairs, a poor attempt to delay the deadline. The two doctors are waiting for her in the office. Jean-Paul gets up when she arrives and leads her to a chair. Her blouse billows in the movement, Eleanor is surprised to see no pants. Would he be naked underneath? That makes her blush.

- Aren't you too stressed?" he asks, avoiding health platitudes.

Eleonora is grateful that he is taking her nervousness into account.

- Oh yes, I am!

- I hope you followed our instructions," interjects Désiré.

- Yes, I ate almost nothing at noon and I haven't eaten anything since.... And I'm so thirsty!

- It will pass as soon as we put in an IV," says Jean-Paul. 'You're planning to stay all night, aren't you? Where's your stuff?

- Um, should we have brought some?

- Never mind, we'll lend you a suit.

Désiré gets up in turn. He's not even wearing pants. Is it because of the hygiene requirements for the next operation?

- Well," he says, "it's time to start the preparation.

- Like... like the day before yesterday?

- Don't you want to?

- Oh yes!... Um... You know what's best for me.

- So take off your clothes.

Eleonora takes off her clothes and folds them on the chair.

- Shall I get on the bed?" she asks, once naked.

- Yes, yes!" nodded Jean-Paul, coming out of the reverie in which he had been immersed by the young girl's striptease.

Désiré helps him get his feet in the stirrups. He is now in charge of the digital part of the preparation. He moves his hand over the girl's stomach, thighs and mound before attempting to insert his middle finger. For his part, Jean-Paul caresses the breasts and manipulates the nipples, which he swells between his fingers. Eleonora moans softly. These almost chaste touches are good for her. She has been waiting for them. Her breathing becomes gentler.

- Yes, there," encourages Desiderio, "relax.

She shudders as he pushes his finger, then another, into her dewy vagina.

- Aaah!

Jean-Paul, without leaving her breasts, pulls a stiff sex out from under her blouse and presents it to Eleanor's hand, which closes on it. She is pleased to guess that the doctors are naked under the blouse.

- Aaah!... Yesii!" she murmurs as Désiré's thumb circles over her clit.

In a convulsive motion, he squeezes the shaft and gently masturbates it. Jean-Paul pulls away. He takes the black doctor's place between her widened thighs and brings the glans to the lips of her enlarged sex.

- Aaah!... Yes!... Come!... Aaaah!

The girl draws the doctor into her dripping pussy.

While his colleague stalks the girl, Désiré prepares the infusion. He attaches his arm to a special holder and punctures the vein. Eleonora, on the verge of orgasm, doesn't even realize that a plastic tube connects her arm to a bottle of serum. Jean-Paul, alternating slow and fast penetrations, brings her to an orgasm, which she had not reached the day before.

- Aaah!... Yes!... Aah!... Yes!... Yes!... Yes!

With the satisfaction of duty accomplished, Jean-Paul ejaculates in a final grunt.

- Arrggghh!... Your turn... Aah!... Desire.

This pushes his colleague who takes too long to release himself and sinks into the still open orifice.

- Mmmh!" moans Eleonora as the big penis spreads the elastic flesh.

The gentle rubbing begins again, the pleasure increases with each coming and going of the sleeve that stretches her belly. Eleonora valiantly resists the blows inflicted. Désiré quickens his pace.

- Hey," Jean-Paul moderates, "take your time, I'm not ready.

The anesthesiologist calms down. His colleague washes his hands.

- Here, you can go," he says after putting on his surgical gloves.

Désiré resumes his kidney strokes. Poor Eleonora no longer knows which way to turn, the lump that is overwhelming her has taken away all her will.

She is nothing but an empty hole that sex fills. With her free arm, she touches her attacker's shoulder. Jean-Paul checks the fixation of his other arm, fiu! It holds well. He prepares the big speculum, the one that had frightened the girl so much, and waits for Désiré to finish his round. From the intensity of the moans, it can't last. There... yes... it's over.

Désiré pulls away. He staggers a little. Now is not the time to back down. She quickly washes her hands while Jean-Paul presents the speculum. Prepared as she is, she won't feel it going in, she thinks. In fact, Eleonora exhales only a weak groan. She is broken. The subsequent orgasms have exhausted her. She doesn't react when Jean-Paul covers her with a sterile sheet and Désiré inserts the EKG leads and puts on the breathing mask...

It is dark when she wakes up. Where is he? He doesn't recognize the doctor's office. He tries to move, one arm is tied. The other is free. He fumbles, touches something wandering at the end of a wire. A door opens, the corridor light faintly illuminates the room? Désiré leans over.

- Oh, you're awake!

Eleonora tries to speak but her mouth is so dry she can't.

- Don't try to speak, just say hello. Are you in pain?

Eleonora shakes her head negatively.

- Good, you're responding well. I'm going to inject you with a sedative that will make you sleep until morning. Let yourself be carried away by your dreams.

The girl doesn't have time to smile before sinking into a deep sleep....

It is Jean-Paul who is at her bedside when she opens her eyelids. She feels fine, no pain. She's not thirsty, just dry-mouthed. She runs her tongue over her lips.

- Drink some of this, it will do you good," she hurries to get a plastic cup half full of water.

Eleonora manages to swallow. Aah! That's better. She smiles at her doctor.

- Did you have a good night? Good. You can go home now, just one last check to make sure everything is okay. Stand up.

She is all surprised to be in scrubs and that her IV is gone. When did they take it out? One little glance...she clings to Jean-Paul who takes her to his office in small steps. He lays her down on the exam table. She puts her feet in the stirrups before he asks.

- Put... Ah! I see you beat me to it. Thank you.

With gentle gestures he dabs the vaginal orifice, introduces a small diameter probe that tickles the girl.

- Well...no bleeding...everything looks good. You can get dressed and go home.

Eleonora finds all her things neatly folded. Jean-Paul gives her a prescription.

- Wear a tampon as if you were menstruating, he advises. Come back in a week for a final checkup, Saturday night at seven for example.

- One last one?" he asks mischievously.

Sigh.

- Until then, no sex, I'm counting on you.

- Yes, doctor.

- Good. Oh, when I think about it, do you have any money on you?

- Uh... yeah, a little.

- Enough to take a cab? It would be safer than taking the subway.

- Um... I think so.

Check her purse.

- Ten... twenty... forty euros...

- I think that will be enough. Good, then we can say goodbye.

- The anesthesiologist isn't here?

- Désiré, no, he's gone home. I'll give him your regards.

- Well...

- What do you want to ask?

- Will he be here next Saturday?

- I'll give him the message," he smiled. I'd be surprised if he didn't show up.

Jean-Paul leads her to the door.

- 'Doctor, don't I owe you anything?

- You're in a public hospital, miss, the treatment is free....

Eleonora found herself in the hallway. On this Sunday morning, it was full of visitors from patients. She didn't want to waste her money on a cab, but the few steps she'd taken from Jean-Paul's office had made her tired.

Taking the subway was out of the question. Ah yes, Maria and her little car. She phones her cousin who has a driver's license and asks her to pick her up at the hospital. Maria eagerly accepts. She will be able to question Eleanor without witnesses during the trip....

CHAPTER 4

On Monday morning, Eleonora feels well enough to go back to school. She is afraid that what she has just done, an abortion, will show on her face. It doesn't. Her friends surround her as usual to talk about what they did over the weekend.

She overhears a conversation about abortion. She listens to see if it's not about her. No, her friends were talking about other girls who have had abortions. Opinions differ on how long it takes to recover, each highlighting the experience they heard about and exaggerating a bit. It ranges from three days to three weeks! On the other hand, everyone insists on post-operative pain:

- Do you think so?" asks Eleonora.

- I assure you, an unbearable pain, my dear, a terrible stomach ache!" says the oldest girl in the class, pointing to the place of pain.

Eleonora looks at her astonished. Isn't she exaggerating? Then she remembers that the girl was absent for a week in the first trimester, for an alleged minor stomach operation. She must be talking about experience, she imagines.

How come she felt almost nothing? Is she numb to pain or is the gynecologist's method the cause? She understood that both doctors had taken advantage of her, but wasn't that the reason for the absence of painful side effects? She smiles inwardly as she remembers Jean-Paul's suggestion to facilitate the introduction of the instruments by vaginal massage. Fun massages! They fucked her, yes! They paid on the beast! But she doesn't blame them. She had so much fun! Especially with Désiré and his big cock.

My God, what an enormity! To think that she accepted him, that he entered her effortlessly! Would it have been the same if Jean-Paul hadn't paved the way? Why not check on the next visit since it's obvious that both operators will make love to her? No, she won't try, she will respect the order, Jean-Paul first, the anesthesiologist with his big sleeve next, he is more cautious.

She will take the pill, once is enough! She hopes Jean-Paul will prescribe it. She also hides a packet of condoms in the bottom of her purse that she and Maria bought at a pharmacy far from their homes.

At school, she tries to guess how big the boys in her class are by the distortion of their jeans. Are they as well-made as Luc or the gynecologist? He doesn't compare them to Désiré, don't dream! "My God!" she says to herself when she realizes where her thoughts are taking her, "am I becoming a nymphomaniac? This is not the time! Jean-Paul has recommended abstinence from sex! He doesn't even dare touch himself in bed at night and there's no talk of fondling Maria!

The week is long and Saturday even longer. At six o'clock her mother announces that she has an appointment.

- Don't wait for me to put you to bed.

- Yes, Mother.

- What are you going to do with your evening?

- I want to go for a walk in the Latin Quarter ... I promise I'll be back soon, she hastened to add when she saw the frown on his face.

- Well, I trust you.

Béatrice Girard was no longer finished getting ready. The line is on tenterhooks ("Will she leave eventually?"), until the front door closes. She waits a few more minutes to make sure she doesn't run into her mother on the subway platform and then heads for the hospital. Seven o'clock is ringing in the chapel bell tower as she crosses the hall. She runs up the stairs and knocks breathlessly on door 303.

- She enters.

Jean-Paul is alone.

- I'm sorry I'm late, Doctor," Eleonora says as she closes the door, "my mother didn't want me to leave.

- There's no harm done, don't worry. Just sit down and calm down. We have plenty of time.

- Isn't your colleague here?

- He'll be here soon. Besides, we don't need him for the first exams. Please undress.

The line is used to this. She takes off all her clothes, carefully folds them on the back of the chair and turns to the gynecologist.

- Should I go to the examination table?

- Ah yes!" says Jean-Paul, who detaches himself from the girl's contemplation with difficulty.

The line stretches across the sheet of paper protecting the table. He approaches her. "He's not wearing pants like last time," she observes, "will he make love to me right away or wait for the other one?" He inserts his feet into the stirrups.

- Not right away," Jean-Paul asks.

He strokes the flat stomach. The line shivers, goose bumps developing under the touch.

- Did you feel no pain? No bleeding?

- No, doctor, not at all. In fact, I've been meaning to ask you, some of my friends have told me it hurts afterwards, is that true?

- It usually does. You say you didn't feel any pain?

- None at all, doctor.

- Good, good! That is a sign that you are recovering well and that the surgery left no side effects. Now you can put your feet in the stirrups.... Yes... I'm going to check the status of your vagina and cervix.

Jean-Paul takes the probe from an endoscope and settles between your open thighs. He is about to insert the device.

- You... are not preparing me? I'll suffer if you don't massage me.

The gynecologist looks at the girl who smiles at him. She is not deceived, he imagines. She is not angry at them for taking advantage of her and asks for more. This takes a huge weight off her stomach. She is consenting and of legal age, no more problems!

- The test I'm going to do is just to see if you can handle a massage. But you're right, a little preparation won't be superfluous.

She places the device down and gently strokes the lips of the vulva, the entrance to the vagina.

- Mmmh!... Mmmh!...

The delicate flower of the girl's sex attracts him irresistibly. He puts his mouth on it.

- Oooh!... Aaah! You surprised me!.... Yes!" she moans, putting her hands on the doctor's hair as he laps at the dew of her vagina.

After a minute, Jean-Paul stands up again, his chin glistening.

- I think I can examine you without any difficulty.

- Aah!... Do it doctor," Eleonora murmurs, rather excited.

The gynecologist introduces the probe that slides easily into the lubricated vagina. She checks the progress on a screen.

- Are you okay, doctor?" asks Eleonora, a little worried by Jean-Paul's silence.

- Everything is perfect, Miss, the operation was a success," he says, removing the device.

- 'Does this mean that you will be able to...? um, massage me?

- You know, Miss, I don't have to give you an additional exam and a vaginal massage is not essential.

- Oh! You don't want to? I'm scared, doctor.

- Of what? There's no reason to be.

- I'm afraid I'll get hurt if I go with a boy. Please doctor, give me a massage now, it will calm me down.

- Under these conditions, I agree to please you.

- Oh, thank you doctor!... Um... Isn't your colleague coming?

- Do you agree?

- Oh yes, I would!

- Very well, I will call him.

While waiting for the anesthesiologist, Jean-Paul prescribes the pill to the girl and advises the use of condoms.

- Erm... I have some in my bag, he admits.

- Very well, you're going to show me how you use them, but first, let me prepare you... er... with my fingers.

- Oh yes, doctor! Get ready!

Désiré caught them fingering the girl and she stroking his penis.

- You should close the door Jean-Paul! What would you have said if a nurse had come in?

- We would have invited her to join us!... Seriously, there is no one left in the ward at this hour, I was waiting for you to arrive. Please close the door.

Désiré turns the key. Jean-Paul takes off his gown, imitated by the anesthesiologist. They are naked underneath. Eleonora admires the unfolded penises. She drools at the thought of receiving them. Jean-Paul's first, Désiré's is definitely too big to begin with.

The gynecologist stands next to the girl. He hands her a condom.

- Show me if you know how to use it.

On the second try, he declares himself satisfied and moves forward between her thighs. He holds the clothed rod in his hand and points it at his target.

- Aaah!... Yes!... Massage me!

The anesthesiologist approaches from the side. He takes the girl's hand and places it on the shaft of her sex. The line cannot be held completely. She slides it slowly, uncovering the glans as he caresses the sensitive breast and Jean-Paul fills it with his loins.

- Aaah!... Yes!... Arrggh!

An orgasm shakes her. Désiré winces, Eleonora has gripped his penis tightly in the grip of pleasure. As a precaution he withdraws. The gynecologist accelerates his penetrations.

- You... Han!... you didn't... Han!...you don't... Han!...you're not hurt?

- No... Aah!... no, you... Aah!... you can... Aah!... keep going... Aah!... the massage!

New orgasm.

- Much better... much better!

Jean-Paul's cum spurts out. Three more strokes and he pulls back. Désiré puts a condom in Eleonora's hands, but she, still under the emotion of pleasure, can't put it on. He does it himself and pushes his big cock into her dilated vagina.

- Aaah!... Yes!... Aaarrrggghhh!

The line can't cum anymore. She thinks she reaches the pinnacle of pleasure with each penetration, but the next one moves her even more. It's much better than she remembers. It must be said that there is no apprehension about the procedure today. All of her energy is focused in her lower abdomen to sustain the extreme pleasure and she no longer has the strength to scream. Only a continuous moan is heard from her tight lips. Jean-Paul, who has put his blouse back on, wipes his sweaty forehead. Désiré increases the pace. One last mumble and he collapses onto the girl.

Jean-Paul checks with a speculum that Eleonora does not feel inserted, that the embrace has left no side effects. Reassured, he gently cleans the sensitive sex. The two men sit in the doctor's office and have a drink while Eleonora recovers.

- Where... where are you?

- We're here," Jean-Paul hurries over. 'I congratulate you, you did very well with the.... um...

- The massage?

- That's right, the massage. Now you can get dressed. The exam is over.

Eleonora, a little shaky, puts on her things. Jean-Paul presents her with a glass of orange juice, which she whistles.

- You have something more... um...

- Invigorating?... Yes, try it!

He hands her a small glass of alcohol.

- Drink slowly.

Eleonora lowers her lips.

- Oh! It's strong!

She feels good in the company of these two men who made her come. They chat quietly. Jean-Paul asks her about the baccalauréat at the end of the year. She admits that she is worried. The two doctors try to reassure her; they are sure it will pass. Désiré announces that he will soon be leaving for Martinique, where he will help set up a cardiac surgery department.

- I'm going to find my family, I miss them, you know.

- Won't you be here for my next visit? By the way doctor, when should I come back?

- Um... In about six months, but this time make an appointment with my secretary. It's safer.

Eleonora takes her leave of the two doctors who embrace her fraternally. Once the girl has left, they pour themselves a glass of cognac.

- Do you have other clients like her?

- Unfortunately not..." Jean-Paul continues after a silence, "You noticed, as I did, the absence of post-operative pain, didn't you?

- Are you suggesting that this is a happy consequence of our shameful maneuvers?

- It would seem so. I can't explain it any other way.

Désiré bursts out laughing.

- What are you laughing about?

- I can imagine the look on our learned professors' faces if we published an article entitled "How to make post-abortion pain disappear" where we developed the method that worked so well with your young Eleonora!

Jean-Paul accompanied her in her hilarity. After rearranging their desks, the two friends part ways and wish each other a good weekend.

In the subway, Eleonora finds a seat. She has to admit to herself that she is a little tired. Sexual excesses must be paid for, she discovers. She doesn't regret the evening. Never in her brief erotic experience had she come so much.

Not even the last night at the chalet when she was fucked by five men. She was convinced that the size of Désiré's cock had something to do with it, just as she was convinced that she wouldn't have had as much pleasure if the black man had fucked her alone. It took the conjunction of two sites, the medium one first, the large one later, to achieve this result.

What a shame the anesthesiologist is leaving! He caught himself trying to guess the sex size of the black men on the train. Are they mounted as well as Désiré? Or is this a rare phenomenon? Will he be able to repeat the experience?

RECREATIONAL AFTERNOONS

CHAPTER 1

Until her graduation, Eleonora remains silent. It's not that her senses are at rest, no! She can't look at a boy without trying to guess if he has a penis as big as Désiré's. But she is too afraid of being disappointed and refuses all invitations to clubs. She can't say why, but she avoids being alone with Maria. She compensates with many solitary caresses in the privacy of her bedroom or bathroom.

After the dreaded exam, she locks herself away in her solitude. She even refuses to attend the general celebration after the long-awaited success. Her mother combines her cousin's prayers with her reproaches.

- You are unreasonable, my dear. You should enjoy yourself and see your friends. You have the whole holiday to prepare for college. Maria complained that you refused to go out with her tonight.

- I don't feel like going out, Mom.

- Look, honey, I hate to leave you alone again. I have to go out. Do me a favor. I'd feel better if you were with friends instead of moping around in front of the TV.

- All right, I accept. I'll call Maria and ask her to pick me up.

- Thank you, my dear, you'll see, you won't regret it.

After much hesitation, Eleonora chose a light dress with a full skirt and a floral blouse over matching orange underwear. She lets her brown hair fall in front of the mirror. She likes the image she sees. Maybe she will meet a handsome man who will make her forget Désiré, it is not forbidden to dream.... The sound of the front door made her jump. Maria already? She wouldn't be here for half an hour. At the second imperative ring of the bell, the line rushed.

- Yes, yes, I'm coming! Oh!

He stopped in astonishment. Bernard Constant, the manager of the ski chalet, was there, smiling.

- Hello Eleonora, don't you recognize me?

- S-s-sir.

- Sir? I seem to remember that you called me by my first name.

- Um... yes, yes, Bernard.

- Aren't you going to invite me in?

- Um... yes, yes! Have a seat.

The director walks into the hall without hesitation.

- Do you... want to see my mother?

- No... Um... Yes. She asked me to come a few days ago, but I could only come this afternoon.

- She's not here. She's out all evening.

- That's too bad, I'm sorry.

No, you're not! Bernard knew very well that Beatrice Girard would be absent. It was her daughter she wanted to see.

- Would you allow me to stay a while and talk to you? Pour me a whiskey, please.

She sat down in a chair and stretched her legs. The girl, too stunned by his impertinence, obeyed.

- Come here, you," she ordered, placing her glass on the empty one Eleanor had brought, "I'm going to have a drink. "'Don't break me,' she insisted in the face of visible disgust. 'You were so kind at the cottage. I dare hope it will be the same here, or else....

The threat worked. At the cottage, the principal had obtained the cooperation of the two girls by threatening to tell their mothers everything. The line approaches the chair. Bernard slid his hand under her skirt and caressed her thighs. He can't suppress the thrill this contact gives him.

- You won't tell Mom, will you?

- Don't worry. If you behave as well as you did at the cabin, you have nothing to worry about... ..... Show me you haven't forgotten how to please me," she says, unzipping her pants and pulling out her stiff sex. "Come on! Hurry up! Be glad I'm not asking you to get naked!

Line chews, kneeling between her spread knees. The shaft rising before her eyes attracts her. It wasn't as big as Désiré's, but it reminded her of Jean-Paul, the gynecologist. She approaches the figure, opens her mouth wide and swallows the head.

- Aah!... Yes! Suck me!

The young girl rediscovers the gestures she thought she had forgotten. She sees herself in the monitor room, licking the living scepter of the director, while Luc and Marc fuck Lucille next to her.

- Aah! Yes!" Bernard sighs. Again!... Yes!... It's better than I remember!... Yes!

Eleonora is proud of her strength. She takes pleasure in manipulating the living stem, in feeling it squirm in her hands. She pumps with application. The sound of the front door made her jump.

- Go on," Bernard orders, but Eleonora refuses.

- But... But it's Maria who's coming for me.

- Maria? Quick, open the door and bring her in!

The young girl hurries inside. She is glad that her cousin interrupts her. She would not be alone with the figure.

- Yes," she answers the surprised look, "we have a visitor.

He leads Mary into the living room.

- Who is it? Oh!

The young girl stopped at the threshold. Bernard is there, Bernard who introduced her to sodomy! Bernard gently strokes his penis to keep it hard. Trembling, she leans against the frame. Mechanically, it handles the stem.

- Yes... That's good... More... Yes, yes, yes. Now the mouth.

Maria has a gag. This is not the introduction she would have chosen. She would much rather feel the cock entering her belly...front or back, whatever.

- No, no, I don't want that.

- What do you mean you don't want to? What do I feel? Would you rather I tell your mother how you behaved at the cottage?

- No, no, please.

- Then obey, faster! Show your cousin that you haven't forgotten anything.

With tears in her eyes, Mary knelt between her open knees. She took her tail in her hands and brought her mouth closer.

- Yes," Bernard encouraged her. .... "Yes!... Lick it well... Yes!... Aah!... You're as good as Eleonora... Yes!... What are you doing? Do you want to continue?" he orders when Maria tries to get up.

- But... Eleonora wants to too...

She hopes to escape the ejaculation.

- It's your fault... You shouldn't have interrupted us, you're the one who's going to take my alcohol. Take my cock again... Yes... Swallow it... Aah!... Yes!

Maria accepts the inevitable. She pumps dutifully, alternating between licking the shaft and sucking the glans, the tip of which is aroused by her tongue.

- Yes!... Up... Aah!... Great!... Aaah!... Coming... Yes!... Aaagghhh!

Bernard bends under the dagger of lust. Maria nearly chokes as her mouth fills. She can't swallow it all and a trickle runs down her lips. Fearing a reprimand, she manipulates the shaft until it loses all stiffness and rests limply on her pants. She jumps to her feet and runs to the bathroom to spit out the excess sperm.

When he returns, Eleonora is sitting on one of Bernard's thighs, which has left his pants. A manager's hand disappears under her flowered skirt.

- Come and sit down, he invites her.... First take off your panties.... Yes, your cousin is naked, do you want to see?

- Um... I believe you.

She takes off her underwear and throws it on a chair, where it joins Eleonora's underwear, which she hadn't noticed when she came back from the bathroom. She walks over. Bernard sits on her other thigh. His hair tickles her groin, making her shiver.

- I am pleased with you," the manager says, flattering her buttocks and caressing the crack with his fingertips.

- You... You won't tell Mom?

- Not if you continue to give me satisfaction.... Caress me... Yes, both of you... I like to feel your hands on my cock.... See how he enjoys it!... Yes... Keep going...

Her middle finger runs between the ladies' buttocks. Maria moves so that her finger reaches her anus. She lets out a sigh of satisfaction when the tip sinks a few millimeters. Eleonora, on the other hand, does all she can to avoid the introduction. Bernard is amused. She is the one who decides to fuck!

- My beautiful line, the arrival of your cousin did not allow you to taste my sperm. You have been victimized. It is only fair that you receive compensation. I'm going to make you cum in my ass, baby.

- Oh no!" he moaned.

- What are you saying? What did you say? I'm sure I didn't hear you right. Aren't we supposed to thank Uncle Bernard for doing his best to please you?

- Um...

- What did you say?" he threatened.

- Thank you, Bernard," she whined.

- That's the spirit! Since I don't want Maria to be jealous, you girls will caress each other while I give pleasure to Eleonora.

She had them remove their skirts and lay on the couch, head to toe, with Maria underneath. He lingers for a few minutes, watching them nibble on each other and maintaining the stiffness of his penis with a distracted caress.

- I see you've made progress. That makes my heart happy. You weren't this good at the cabin.... Well, now it's my turn.... Maria, lick my glans, I don't want to hurt your cousin... Yes, there... Good... Help me spread my buttocks... Thank you... I insert a wet finger... I twist it to soften the muscle... There... Do you feel how nice it is, Eleonora?

- Um...

- Keep sucking, you! Tell Maria. Well, I think the preparation will be enough. I put the glans against the disk... I push .... Han!

- Ouch!

- No, no, it doesn't hurt, does it? Caress yourself well... Yes... You'll see, Eleonora, how beautiful it is!

Bernard pushes the penis up to the guard.

- Mmmh!" moans Eleonora.

Little by little, she regained the pleasant sensations she had discovered in the hut. She works on her cousin's clit, which responds to her caresses.

Watching the cock move in and out of her dilated anus makes Maria shudder with envy. Why didn't Bernard choose her instead of forcing her to perform oral sex? Suddenly she stiffens: Eleonora had just inserted a piece of nail into the small hole. She reacts by inserting two fingers into her vagina. She enjoys the feeling of the lump going in and out of the nearby duct, happy that her cousin is imitating her by piercing her two orifices.

Bernard pushes the penis up to the guard.

- Mmmh!" moans Eleonora.

Little by little, she regains the pleasant sensations she had discovered in the hut. She works on her cousin's clit, which responds to her caresses.

Watching the cock move in and out of her dilated anus makes Maria shudder with envy. Why didn't Bernard choose her instead of forcing her to perform oral sex? Suddenly she stiffens: Eleonora had just inserted a piece of nail into the small hole. She reacts by inserting two fingers into her vagina. She enjoys feeling the lump going in and out of the nearby duct, happy that her cousin is imitating her by piercing her two orifices.

Bernard speeds up his pace. He holds his victim by the hips and hits her with his kidneys. The line is shaken. Afraid of hurting Mary, he stops his caresses and resumes them only when the director gets up with loud moans. The two girls do not get up when the man withdraws and leaves them for a quick wash.

He finds them in the same place and waits in the chair until their desire for pleasure has subsided.

- I'm sorry Maria," he smiled, waving his flaccid penis, "but my personal resources do not allow me to honor you in turn as you deserve. I promise you'll be at the party next time.

- You... Will you come back?

- Wouldn't you like that?

- Uh... yes," Eleonora answers without conviction.

- Well, I like to make the people around me happy.... Well, there's no point in continuing," she said, releasing her desperately limp sex. I'm done for the next few hours. It's a shame I have to leave you, my darlings, and I can't wait for my strength to return.

He gets up and puts on his underwear and pants. The girls put their skirts back on.

- It's a pity, I liked to see you with your buttocks in the air. Well, one can't have everything... No! Not the panties! Stay naked... at least while I'm here! Give us a drink, Eleonora... Yes, whiskey. Don't you want some?

The girls help themselves to orange juice. They look at each other with their eyes. What does Bernard still want? Isn't it over?

He finally puts down his glass.

- Aah! That's better! That's not all, I came with a specific purpose, but when I saw you, I got carried away and couldn't resist the pleasure of pleasing you ladies. I said that I'm giving a little party on Tuesday afternoon and I'd like to invite you.

Eleonora turned pale. What kind of party? A repeat of last night at the cottage? Bernard's expressionless face tells her nothing.

- Um...

- I'm counting on you.

- Um...

- I'll be very disappointed if you don't come.... Very disappointed... To the point of complaining...

Eleonora sighs heavily. The threat is accurate, but she doesn't know if she would rather face her mother's wrath than relive the sex orgy of the last night of vacation. Not that she didn't enjoy it.

She still trembles with desire when she thinks back to the multiple orgasms that rocked her, but she is left with a feeling of disgust, a shame that she behaved like a lustful beast. She has only good memories of her encounters with the gynecologist, perhaps because there were only two? Look at Maria, as pale as she is.

- You disappoint me," continued Bernard when he saw that the girls were not making up their minds.

- For pity's sake," begs Maria, "don't tell our mothers.

- It's up to you.

- Um... it's in the afternoon, you say?

- Yes, so you don't have to ask permission. I promise you'll be free by eight o'clock. Can I count on you?

- Or... yes. Right, Eleonora?

Unable to say a word, she nodded. On her own, she would have refused, despite the predictable consequences, but there's her cousin... .... Bernard scribbled a business card.

- Here's the address you need to go to and the access code. I'll expect you there on Tuesday at two in the afternoon, it's on the fifth floor.... Absolutely, right?

- Um... what should we wear?

- You look perfect in those clothes, ladies. Well, I'll leave you to it, I still have a lot of work to do to get everything organized.

He gets up. Maria accompanies him to the door. He holds her against him, flattering her bottom under her skirt.

- See you Tuesday afternoon.

He meets Eleonora in the living room.

- Do you think we should go? she asks. Aren't you afraid it'll be like in the hut?

- No, I'm not! Not in the afternoon... well... er... I think... er... I... I don't know... ..... Do you think we should have said no?

- You're right, maybe I'm worrying for nothing.

You put the glasses away.

- Weren't we going out?" asks Maria.

- It's late now. Her friends must have left.

Actually, Eleonora is afraid that everyone will read in her face that she enjoyed sucking Bernard's cock, and she imagines that she won't have the strength to withdraw if one of Maria's friends asks her for the same service.

Maria approaches her cousin and kisses her on the neck.

- Don't you want us to caress each other?

The line yields. Yes, she does, a raging desire. She takes the pleading figure and crushes her mouth under her lips....

CHAPTER 2

Two in the afternoon. Eleanor looks at the address and compares it to the note Bernard gave her. This is it. A plush building, reassuring in the summer light. She dials the entry code. The door opens slowly.

- Are you entering?

Maria hesitates.

- I'm afraid...

With her back against the wall, she is no longer sure whether to give in to Bernard or suffer her mother's rage. The consequences of each eventuality frighten her. Eleonora, on the other hand, has passed this stage. She reluctantly accepted the meeting, but now she is taking responsibility.

- It's no longer time to procrastinate, are you coming or not?

- Um...

Seeing her cousin unable to decide, she pulls her in. Maria watches the door close. The click of the latch as it clicks back into place sounds like the death knell of her youth. Nothing will ever be the same, she feels it. She lets herself be led toward the elevator. The two girls don't say a word during the interminable ascent.

Lucille, the young instructor of the chalet, is waiting for them on the doorstep of the apartment.

- Come in-you're right on time, that's good.

The young woman closes the padded door before hugging her two cousins.

- It's good to see you again. I was happy to hear you were coming. I haven't forgotten the good times we had together during our ski vacation.

The two girls look at each other, trembling. Their fears become clearer. Lucille's suggestions are transparent; the afternoon promises to be hot. On the other hand, they are relieved by this presence, from which they draw comfort.

- Come and say hello to Bernard and his guests.

The young instructor pushes them into a large room filled with armchairs and sofas. Bernard introduces them to a young woman and the various men accompanying her. There are doctors, lawyers, engineers. Maria blushes when a handsome man in his forties kisses her hand. Lucille and the other woman, Daphne, pass around drinks. They hire the two cousins to serve petits fours. After half an hour, the two girls, somewhat titillated by the alcoholic beverages, relax and enjoy circulating among these gallant men who know how to turn a compliment so well.

After the arrival of two new participants, at a sign from Bernard, Lucille approaches Eleonora and Maria and takes them by the hand. The director calls for silence.

- Madam, ladies and gentlemen, we are all here. Our afternoon recreation can begin.

A murmur of approval goes around the male audience, who take their seats in the armchairs and sofas. Eleonora would like to sit down too, but Lucille holds her down. There are ten men besides Bernard.

- As an aperitif," she continued, "Daphne, Lucille, Eleanor, and Maria, our gracious representatives of the fairer sex, will treat us to a dance.... Um... I beg your pardon," he interrupted himself before the gestures of Eleanor and Maria, "but first I must speak to our two new recruits. Daphne and Lucille will serve you drinks. It will only take a few minutes.

Bernard leads the two cousins into a room. Pif! Paf! A slap to each of them.

- Last warning! You agree to behave like a responsible person or I will tie you up on this bed where all the men present will come to fuck you! You can choose between spending a few pleasant hours in good company, or being forced to put up with males who will be displeased with your attitude, not to mention the wrath of your mothers, who I will be happy to inform of your conduct.... So? What's your decision?

- Do you want us to have a strip-tease? Like in the cottage?" asks Eleonora.

- That's all I ask.

- Uh... Maria and I didn't quite understand. Please excuse us.

- Can I count on your full participation? Isn't that Maria?

- Um...yes.

- Well, let's go back to the room and I hope your performance will ease the embarrassment of your exit.

The two cousins return, blushing to be the center of attention in the assembly. Bernard turns on a stereo. A soft harmony fills the living room.

- Ladies, over to you!

Daphne and Lucille each lead a girl in a lascivious dance. After a few steps, the older girl unbuttons Eleonora's blouse and spreads the sides over her white bra. Lucille imitates her and Maria. The cousins realize what is expected of them and their blouses end up on the spectators' knees. A few lines later, it's the turn of the skirts. The four women in their underwear caress each other as they dance. The line breaks first and kisses Daphne. Bernard's sign of encouragement fills her with pride. The bras disappear, the caresses increase, and the tension builds as the first underwear, Mary's, is held aloft by one of the assistants as a trophy. At the end of the dance, the quartet greets the applauding audience.

- Thank you, thank you for our dancers. They will now offer you refreshments. Make yourselves comfortable, gentlemen," Bernard announces.

The four women are besieged by caresses, Eleonora and Maria in particular. Each man present wants to be the first to receive the favors of one of the two newcomers. Bernard has to tidy up a bit.

- Gentlemen, gentlemen, let's see. What will these young beauties think if you fight? And don't forget that the rules of our entertainment, which you all agreed to, require protection.

Bernard puts a packet of condoms on the living room table.

- I remind you of another article in these rules that gives young women participating for the first time the honor of choosing the first knight themselves. But don't worry, the afternoon is not over and I'm sure our ladies will make it a point of honor to please all of you, won't you, my darlings? But please, each of you in turn, Lucille and Daphne will keep you waiting.

Give Eleanor and Maria a condom.

- Choose... no, not me," he whispers to Maria who looks at him insistently, "I'm out of the game.

Eleonora turns to her nearest neighbor, a way of making it clear that she has no preference.

- What should we do?" she asks.

- Come and sit here," she replies pointing to her thigh.

Maria turns before walking toward a mustachioed 40-year-old man, the one who kissed her hand when she arrived. Lucille and Daphne, condom in hand, begin to undress their partner of the moment. The other men wait their turn, running their hands over the naked bodies. Eleonora manages to remove her companion's pants. Kneeling down, she releases the cock that stiffens after three strokes of the wrist. She places a kiss on the tip, pulls the foreskin and licks the glans with her tongue. A murmur of approval runs through the people around her. "Happy initiative," she hears. She meets the eyes of Bernard, who smiles and encourages her; she blushes with pleasure.

Maria has already wrapped "her" penis in latex without undressing the owner. She climbs on her thighs, guides the shaft and impales herself on it. She doesn't have to make any effort: her hands support her and move her up and down the fleshy shaft.

Lucille and Daphne, more experienced, make the pleasure last. They take off the clothes of those around them and present all the parts of their bodies to their greedy mouths.

Eleonora, on all fours on a couch, is taken from behind while a rod is introduced into her mouth. Lucille, spread-legged on an armchair, is fucked by a short, hairy brunette as she masturbates two cocks, and Daphne, between them, satisfies two participants with double penetration.

Maria, who is done with the first one, is taken away by a tall blond man who throws her backwards onto a couch. Bernard has just enough time to slip a condom over his penis, which finds its way between her buttocks, which are spread by caring hands.

- Aahouuh!

- Gentlemen, gentlemen, no brutality, please have mercy on the youth of our friends, the organizer calms him down.

- Da... sorry... Aah!... sorry the offender, I didn't mean to.... Aah!...to hurt you.... Aah!... hurt you.

- It's... it's nothing," stammered Maria who, once the glans was inserted, began to enjoy the friction.

Eleonora's rider ejaculates with a grunt like a satiated wild beast. He is immediately replaced. The girl doesn't notice the change, busy swallowing the semen that fills her mouth. Lucille and Daphne take turns changing partners. Bernard takes care of everything, especially that the fuckers put on condoms before introduction.

Calm returns. Daphne and Lucille lead the two cousins into the bathroom. The gentlemen recover by drinking their cocktails. The comments are going well.

The obvious pleasure shown by the two cousins has satisfied their partners and the others are eager to take their turn. Bernard advises everyone to take their clothes off because he says the fun is just beginning. The young women are enthusiastically welcomed into the main room. The two cousins are very close.

- It's not fair, Monsieur René," Bernard interjects when Maria's first escort wants her to sit next to him. Don't be selfish, think of your colleagues who didn't get your chance.

He places Lucille in his arms.

The second round lasts longer than the previous one, the two cousins transport their admirers with joy with their screams and moans of pleasure and when calm returns, each man has taken his shot in a vagina, an ass or a mouth.

Four participants forfeit in the third round and watch the exploits of their tougher counterparts with pulled faces. Only two finish to fuck Eleonora and Maria for a fourth round.

Seven p.m. Bernard closes the door on the last visitor. He is satisfied. Everything went according to plan, and the little incident at the beginning that forced him to give Eleonora and Maria a run for their money was of no consequence.

- A beautiful afternoon, isn't it? Who should we thank?

The two cousins, slumped in an armchair, do not answer. They don't know how many men they've satisfied, eight? Nine? Daphne and Lucille, who are less stressed, are in better shape. They get up and surround Bernard. He lets them undress him. Invited by the two elders, Eleanor and Mary join the caresses but do not compete for the honor of being fucked. Daphne receives the organizer's homage in her ass, which after a few minutes is pumped by Lucille.

- Well, that's not all, says Bernard, once everyone has showered and dressed, I have to give you the schedule for the next few days.

He takes them to an office and consults his computer.

- Daphne, can you come tomorrow night?.... Yes?... Okay. I'll sign you up.

- Who will I be with?

- With... um... I... I don't know yet," she adds, looking at Eleonora and Maria. I'll give you a call. Lucille, my beautiful, I need you Thursday afternoon.

- Oh no, you don't! Not this Thursday. I'm sorry, my parents are visiting. Can I switch with Daphne?

Bernard turns to Daphne, who nods in agreement.

- 'Well... 'You,' he says, turning to the two cousins after correcting his schedule, 'I'll expect you Saturday afternoon, here, at the same time.

The girls understand that you can't refuse or argue!

- I will go to your house tomorrow, Maria, I must speak to you.

- Can't we do it now?

- No, it's too late.

- But mother will be there.

- Don't worry, I'll be discreet, she won't suspect anything. I want to talk to you too, Eleonora. Be at your cousin's at three o'clock, understand?

The four women parted on the sidewalk. Lucille and Daphne came by car, the cousins took the subway.

- Do you think Saturday will be the same?" asks Maria when they get on the train.

The line doesn't answer. What's the point! It's obvious! Saturday and the following days! She is convinced that Bernard will not let them down soon.

- If your mother and mine do not suspect anything, I will die!

The line remains silent.

CHAPTER 3

The next day Eleonora rings Maria's doorbell. She didn't want to come. What a way to pass the time! Bernard should not imagine that he can demand everything!

She went out for a walk, promising herself not to go to her aunt's house, but as if she had done it on purpose, at five to three she turned into the avenue and a few minutes later stopped in front of the door trembling with apprehension and impatience.

She realized that he had not taken advantage of her or her companions the day before while there were visitors.

What would Bernard ask? He hasn't fucked her so far, settling for her ass and mouth.

He rings the door bell.

- Enter, it's open!

Bernard's voice! He enters his aunt's house.

- Please lock the door again.

She obeys. From the hallway, she has a view of the living room. Maria, completely naked, is kneeling between the man's open knees. The up and down movements of her head betray her occupation.

- Get undressed... Faster than that and reach your cousin.... Everything!" he orders when Eleonora, in her underwear, pretends to approach.... Good, come and help Maria.

She eagerly gives in. It's not in her mouth that Bernard will ejaculate, so much the better! Eleonora, docile, takes the quivering penis in her hand and licks it with small strokes.

- Aah! It is a pleasure to be sucked by such beautiful people!

She pulls Maria's hair, forces her to stand up and pulls her against herself.

- Keep sucking me, you!" he says to Eleonora, who is working on the stiff shaft.

She squeezes the nipple close between her lips.

- Aaah!

72

The girl pushes her breast forward. Bernard's hand moves down to her buttocks, into her slit. A fingernail scratches her anus and tries to enter.

- Aaah!" Maria sighs as she moves to get the finger in.

The line swallows the glans to extract the seed.

- Slowly my beautiful, slowly.... Mmmh!... Yes!... Aah!

Suddenly, Bernard stands up and pushes Maria down against the couch. He guides his salivating cock between her buttocks. The girl, who has figured out what he wants, slams her ass.

- Line! Help her!

Although she was disappointed to see her toy escape her, she pulls on the lobes of her buttocks and protrudes her anus. The director puts the tip of his sex into it. He pushes.

- Aaah!

Double groan as the glans sinks in and disappears from view.

- Stroke her at the same time, he orders, amplifying her loins.

Eleonora slips her hand under Maria's belly and enjoys titillating the sensitive button.

- Aaah!... Yesii!... Again!... Yesii!

- Do you like... han!... taking... han!... hole... han!... washing machine.

- Yes!

- Say... han!... that you like... han!... my cock.

- Yes!

- Say it...han!

- I love... ah... your cock.

- Where?

- I love... Aah!...your cock... Aah!...inside... Aah!... in the ass... Aaah!

- Aaagghh!

Bernard gives the last licks before slumping down on Maria's back. Eleonora pushes him away and frees her cousin, whom she drags into the bathroom.

When they return, the man wipes his sex with tissues.

- I'm sorry, Eleonora, for disappointing you today. I still have Lucille and Daphne to visit, so I have to take it slow. I promise next time I'll devote myself completely to you.... Can you hand me my briefcase?

He opens it and pulls out two envelopes.

- This is for you, Eleonora, and for you, Maria," he said, handing them to the two girls.

- What is this?" asks the latter.

- Open it and you'll see.

- Oh!" he exclaimed when he discovered the notes, "one, two, three, four, five! Five hundred... er... four hundred and fifty euros! Why?

- That's the reward for your participation, minus the fifty euro fine for forcing me to do a turnaround. You'll have all this every afternoon.

- Next Saturday too?

- Saturday and the following days.

- Did you hear that, Eleonora? We'll be able to afford anything we want! Thank you Bernard!

The girl jumps on the director's neck and gives him two resounding kisses.

- Well, all right, all right. The best thanks will be to behave yourself when I ask you to come.

He picks up his underwear and pants.

- I'm leaving you. Like I said, I have to stop by Lucille and Daphne's.... No, you don't have to get dressed, I like seeing you like this, and besides, Maria, I'm counting on you to make up for Eleonora. She's been bullied, make her come. I'm asking as a favor.

The line is blurred.

- Do you realize what this means?" she said, waving the envelope she hadn't opened when they closed the door.

- Aren't you happy?

- We're prostitutes!

- No, we're not! We don't walk the streets.

- What do you call taking money for sex?

- We didn't ask for it! It's a gift. Oh! Then do what you want! I'm keeping it.

Maria ran to her room and put the envelope in the nightstand drawer.

- Aren't you afraid your mother will find out?" asked Eleonora, who had followed her.

- You're right, I have to hide it.

She slips the package into a file on her desk. Her cousin hugs her from behind and caresses her breasts.

- I'm sorry about before, I didn't mean to upset you.... You didn't have to make me come?

Maria turns around and stretches her lips....

- What are you going to do with all that money?" asked Eleonora, getting dressed.

- 'I don't know... I do! I'm going to buy the pretty dress I saw in a store window.

- I don't want my aunt or mom to see it, they might ask questions.

- You're right, I'll be careful. What about you?

- Me? I'll save it for later.

The two cousins separate.

- Will I see you before Saturday?" asks Eleonora, kissing Maria.

- I don't think so. We meet at the entrance of the building at two?

- If you like.

Saturday's session is very similar to the early afternoon. The same number of male guests, the same discretion of Bernard who refrains from participating, the same success of the two cousins who bravely undergo eight or nine successive hugs, the same fatigue at the end of the session. Only their two female partners are different. They had never seen Renée and Josiane before. Later, they are called together once or twice a week. They learn to take it easy, to simulate pleasure instead of letting go.

During the month of August, Bernard has them attend separately, but they meet again together in one or the other house for the distribution of envelopes preceded by a lollipop or sodomy or both when he is fit.

Eleonora doesn't ask any more questions, she accepts the situation. Is she selling her charms? So what? She's not the first! Aside from one time when she didn't make it, she hasn't turned down any of Bernard's dates.

She doesn't mind offering her body in front of and behind participants during recreational afternoons as Bernard calls them. She has known many penises, she sighs, short, long, thin, thick, but none of them have reached the proportions of Désiré's. When will he have this chance?

...It was in September, in the middle of the afternoon, while she was being sodomized, that she saw him....

CHAPTER 4

In her surprise, Eleonora forgets to suck the penis in her hand. Its owner is not satisfied and pushes it into the girl's mouth.

She overcomes the nausea reflex and works on the shaft.

Let's get this over with quickly. She doesn't seem to care what's going on in his ass, he's used to it.... All she cares about is unloading him into her mouth as fast as she can. He comes... Yes, the penis was quivering.... The thin shaft swelled in her hand.... And... Is it there?..

Yes! Eleonora swallowed the sperm with the satisfaction of a fulfilled duty. The satiated man withdrew from her field of vision.

It's still there! Desiré's cock! Huge, just like he sees it in his dreams. And he's not dreaming! It's the same cock that Denise, a woman her mother's age, is licking but can't take in her mouth, but it's not Désiré at the other end. What's his name? Ah, yes, Ahmed. From what she understands, he's an IT guy, probably as rich as any of the guests.

The man fidgets behind him. Is that one not finished yet? Ah, finally! The line feels like a release, the jets of semen swelling the condom. She thanks her date with a wide smile and removes the latex, which she takes into the bathroom and tosses in the trash. She looks in the mirror and finds herself beautiful. She rushes to Ahmed and his gorgeous cock.

She gets stuck in the doorway. She hasn't paid much attention to this man, only surprised by his youthfulness that stands out among the middle-aged participants, but she's sure he hasn't gotten laid yet. Her companions must have been afraid of being ripped apart. Maybe he's afraid of pain? She remembers that it was only after having sex with Dr. Jean-Paul that Désiré was able to push himself into her vagina. He had to prepare himself. Yes, with a normal cock...er...no, not normal, larger than average but still smaller in diameter than the enormity she had seen and wanted to receive.

She walks back into the large room without paying attention to Bernard's dark gaze that scolds her for her absence. Ah, this is what she's looking for. A good-sized cane. She approaches its possessor, slumped in an armchair, with a glass in his hand. The man thanks her and invites her to sit next to him. The line hurries to obey. She manipulates the still soft appendage. A few moments later, she is proudly holding a stiff cane that she covers with latex. She sits on her knees and inserts the device into her eager pussy and begins a frenzied dance. Next to her, Denise places a tissue over Ahmed's cock and masturbates the shaft with both hands. The tissue rises under the pressure of the jets, the man moans and falls back in his chair.

Eleonora tells herself that she must not make her partner cum too soon to give her target time to recover. She calms her pelvic thrusts and lets her partner kiss her breasts. Impatience makes her tremble. Imagining that in a few minutes a cock as big as Désiré's, which she remembers so well, will spread the lips of her sex, filling her pussy, almost brings her to orgasm. Her vaginal muscles dilate on their own, hardly feeling the penis piercing her. She struggles to maintain this comatose state of well-being. She meets Ahmed's eyes. He follows the direction of Eleanor's eyes to her sex. Smiling, she gently caresses it.

The girl moves up and down her partner's thighs without taking her eyes off the penis she craves and which is now reaching its full size. She shudders as the man chooses a good sized condom and dresses the cock. Oh, quick! Let the man who is fucking her finish! She quickens her pace. Aah! Yes! The sperm expands the latex. Two more strokes of the pelvis, the penis becomes smaller.

Eleonora, contrary to her habits, does not let her partner caress her. She rises to place her sex on top of the bulky scepter. A chill runs through the assembly. To enter or not to enter? There is silence in the room, almost all eyes are on the couple, or rather the sex that is shedding flesh. The spectators hold their breath. The acorn crosses the passage and the tree disappears.

- Aaah!

Eleonora's sigh of satisfaction releases the tension in the room. Some applause breaks out. The young girl has no more strength to rise. Ahmed holds her close to him. He gets up, carries her without disuniting and puts her on a free couch and starts the love dance. Eleonora moans continuously. It's as good as she remembers it.

Better yet. The tug in her belly turns into a beneficial wave that sweeps over her. Someone is caressing her breast. This simple gesture opens the floodgates of pleasure. The orgasm increases, impetuous.

- Aaahgggh!

A murmur goes through the audience. Conversations resume around the couple. Bernard, who was absent at the beginning of the embrace, approaches worriedly. He must not let this strangeness ruin his protégé. The girl's visible pleasure only half reassures him. It's hard for him to intervene if she doesn't complain; the participants wouldn't understand. He serves everyone a drink, reserving the right to reprimand the offender in private at the end of the afternoon.

Ahmed melts with pleasure. This is the first time a woman has come in his arms like this. For the first time, he does not feel the size of his sex as a handicap. His previous partners had never expressed such pleasure. She discovers that she can vary the penetrations, alternating back and forth with periods of rest during which the massage of her vaginal muscles envelops his cock with gentle pressure. How beautiful the act of love is when partners join in pleasure! He is in no hurry to finish. He wishes this wonderful embrace would last for hours.... Unfortunately, the pleasure is too strong. He can't control the surge. He collapses, drained, happy. He feels himself being pulled by the shoulders and finds himself sitting on the carpet behind the back of the man who has taken his place, staring blankly at a pair of balls dancing before his eyes.

The emptiness caused by the disappearance of Ahmed's penis did not wake Eleonora from her blissful stupor. She suffers two almost unconscious hugs one after the other before being led to the bathroom by Denise.

- Well, I'll be damned! What a kick! It's been a long time since I've seen someone come like you! Anyway, you should take it easy, my dear. It's not good to exert yourself like that.

- I... I know, but I couldn't help myself.

- How did you put up with this phenomenon? I, tried it once. It hurts! Worse than childbirth! Since then, I've been careful and only masturbated him. Let me check to make sure he didn't hurt you.

- No, I don't think so.

- I insist. Bernard asked... 'I can't believe it,' she murmured after inspecting the horse. 'You're just a little congested. Come on, let's go deliver the good news.

The guests have left the room, including Ahmed. Eleonora is sorry, she would have liked to chat with him, why not exchange addresses. Bernard calls her.

- What unconsciousness! You are unconscious, I swear! You gave me a scare! I gave you a hard time about your rapist, I forbade him to come back!

- But he didn't hurt me... I assure you.

Denise confirms with a glance.

- Well, I admit it. It's good that there are no side effects, but don't let that stop you from taking precautions in the future. I'll book you for the day after tomorrow.

- Um... Can't I have an extra day off?

- What the hell... Okay, you've been working a lot lately. I'll ask Maria to cover for you. We'll decide on a date when I come to your house. In the meantime, get some rest.

CHAPTER 5

With her mother out on an errand, Eleanor waits feverishly for Bernard's visit. She is never reassured when he arrives; her mother could show up at any moment. She envies Maria's relaxed attitude as she begins to undress.

- Do as I do," she invites, "we'll have more time to spend with him. If memory serves me right, it's your turn to suck him off and he needs to have time to recover because I don't have the guts to wait until next week to get fucked.... Come on! Do this for me, I will stroke you while I wait for him.

Eleonora makes some drinks and then consents to her cousin's prayer. She removes her clothes and sits down next to Maria. The two girls share a long kiss while caressing each other's breasts. The sound of the bell interrupts them.

- Who is it?" asks Eleonora.... "Oh, I'll let you in... Yes, it's him," she replies to Maria's questioning look.

They walk together to the hallway and open the door as soon as they hear the sound of the elevator.

- Oh, how nice of you to receive me like this, you deserve a kiss!

Bernard happily hugged the two girls, led them into the living room and sat down between them. They unfasten their shirts and belts. Maria pulls down her pants while Eleonora pulls his penis out of his briefs and kisses the tip.

- Yes! I love the way you take care of me.... Aah!" she sighs as the girl takes the glans into her mouth.

She closes her eyes as she caresses Maria's buttocks.

- Did that hurt, Eleonora?

She shakes her head in denial.

- Why would it hurt?" asks Maria.

- Didn't she tell you? The thoughtless little girl had a dick shoved in her too big for her little pussy.

- No, I'm telling you it didn't hurt!" announces Eleonora as she withdraws her penis...I assure you.

- Well, I admit it... Please continue... Aaah!... Your mouth is so soft!

- Better than my butt?" asks Maria a little jealous.

- Aaah!... Don't ask me... Mmmh!... Choose between the two of you.... Mmmh!

To calm her down, he inserts his finger into her separation. The girl turns her ass over to ease the introduction. The line works on the cock. She knows better by now. She knows how to keep the pleasure going, make it last for the director's ultimate satisfaction. All caught up in her task, she doesn't hear the front door open on Beatrice.

Eleonora's mother stops on the threshold of the living room. Bernard signals to her to be quiet and to Maria who wanted to greet her aunt. Beatrice sighs. She has known for a long time, even from the beginning, how Bernard uses his daughter, but it is hard for her to remain calm when she sees her naked performing fellatio. Until this hour, it was possible for her to close her eyes. She suspects that Bernard sent her to get the flyers on purpose so that she would discover them when he returned and force mother and daughter to face the truth. A month ago, he had already managed to convince her and her sister-in-law Jeannine to catch him sodomizing Maria. Since then, Maria often participates with her or her mother in recreational sessions while keeping her daughter's secret.

Eleanor realizes that Bernard and Maria's attitude has changed. She looks up and sees her mother smiling at her.

- Oh!

She jumps to her feet. Bernard, who was expecting her reaction, manages to hold her back and forces her to sit next to him.

- Hi Beatrice... You stay put!

- Hi Aunt", says Maria.

- Hello everyone, I hope I'm not disturbing you.

- It's you," replied Bernard. You could have waited a few minutes before entering to let your daughter finish what she had started so well.

Eleonora, torn between the shame of being caught in an embarrassing position and the amazement caused by the strange behavior of Maria and her mother, did not know how to behave. She decides not to move.

- I'm sorry, it was involuntary," says her mother.

- I can take your place", offers Maria.

- No, it's your bottom I want to honor. Get into position... Yes, on this couch.

The girl kneels on the bench and rests her chest against the backrest.

- Yes, spread your thighs.... Better than that... Good, let me moisten my finger at your source.

- Aah!

- I'm wetting the little hole...

- Aah!

- There, that's it, we can go... Line, Beatrice! Help me out here.

- Ask her.

- Spread her buttocks.

This is not the first time she has asked for this service. Eleonora is so stunned that she mechanically obeys. Her mother sits on the other side of Maria. Their hands brush against each other on her bottom. Bernard moves her sex forward and guides it with his hand. He caresses her anus before pushing in effortlessly.

- Aaah! yes!" cries the girl.

Beatrice changes sides and sits next to Eleonora, whose shoulder she wraps an arm around. The girl bursts into tears.

- Sorry, mom, sorry.

- You don't have to apologize... Yes, I knew," she adds in front of the questioning look.

- Did you... knew it? Why didn't you say anything?

- I didn't want to hurt your feelings, my dear.

- And you also knew about Maria...

- Yes, your... Aah!... Your mother and mine are.... Aah!... they are aware of it," said the latter, battered by Bernard's blows that the conversation did not prevent from fucking the girl.

- I was the only one who didn't know. You made fun of me.

- But no my dear, but no.

Beatrice pampers her daughter's hair.

- We didn't know... Aah!...how to.... Aah!... tell you," Maria admits.

- It couldn't... han!... last longer... han!... I decided to.... han!... to cut out the abscess," Bernard interjected. Hand... han!... now... han!... let me... han!... finish with this... han!... ma'am. I have other...han!...things to.... han!... do that... han!... listen... han!... you.

- Yes!" echoed Maria.

- Aaaah!... Aaagghhh!

- Yes!... arrmmmh!

The man withdraws his penis. Beatrice takes out a handkerchief and dries it.

- Go rinse off in the bathroom, orders his niece.

She inspects the couch, no stains, lucky for her.

- Next time, Eleonora, use a cloth to protect.

Next time? Does her mother want me to do it again? Eleonora looks at her astonished.

- Beatrice my beautiful, give me my briefcase...thank you.... Here are your envelopes.

She hands them out to Eleonora, Maria who has returned in the meantime and Beatrice.

- You... you too, mom?

- Yes, my little Eleanor, your mother is one of my long-time protectors. Almost a pioneer with your aunt.

- Did you know that?" the young girl asked her cousin.

- I've already taken part in sessions with them," she admits.

- I'm glad the situation has been cleared up," says Bernard, getting dressed. It will make it easier for me to keep my schedule. I won't have to juggle anymore to keep you from meeting.

The line is stunned. Her mother a prostitute! And allowing her daughter to be one! She feels like everything is falling apart around her. A sudden nausea shakes her and she rushes to the bathroom. Upon her return Bernard, with his laptop on his lap, informs her of his new program.

- Eleanor, my dear, it's time to go to the parties. I'll sign you up for next Saturday with your aunt, then Monday afternoon you can go with Maria....

- No!

- What do you mean "no"? You don't want to work with Maria? You're going to hurt your cousin's feelings.

- Not with Maria, not with my aunt or anyone else! Not on Saturday or Monday or any other day of the week! No, not anymore!

Plaf! Bernard slaps the girl hard, who looks at him with round eyes and runs off to her room.

- No, but... Do you think you can leave me like this? Go get her, Beatrice.

- Leave her, please. She is upset and needs rest. We'll talk about it later. Can't you do without her?

- Provided that you, Jeanine and Maria work extra hours to compensate for her absence.

- Will I earn more then?

- Five hundred euros per session, that's the rate. Let's say Maria has a party with her mother on Saturday. You'll find Lucille and Sylvette, okay?.... Well, on Monday, Beatrice, you'll go with your niece with Daphne and Isabelle.... OK?... It's because she's your daughter that I'm so accommodating," he continued, correcting on his computer. Try not to let the situation continue. I would be very disappointed to lose an element, very disappointed....

Bernard leaves them with this veiled threat. Maria approaches her aunt.

- Will she be back soon, Eleonora?

- I don't know... You should get dressed and go home to rest. It will be a busy week.

Left alone, Beatrice hesitates to reach her daughter. What should she tell her? How to tell her that she had been naive enough to believe that Bernard would spare her daughter during winter sports week? How can she be forgiven for her cowardice when he told her at the beginning of the vacation that Eleonora and Maria were part of his flock? She should have rebelled immediately, talked to her daughter and left this pimp, yes he is a pimp, even though he never abused them. To think she obeyed him when he asked her to make it easier for him to get out! Jeannine was of little help to him, she who had understood from the beginning and accepted the situation. 'What the girls earn is just as little to spend on the house,' he replied when Beatrice became indignant. She also pointed out that Maria gave her part of her bonuses: a contribution to household expenses, she said.

Eleonora sobbed on her stomach on the bed. Beatrice approached and stroked her hair.

- Forgive me, my dear, forgive me. I should have protected you, I wasn't able to.

- Did you... Did you know?

- It hasn't been long since Bernard confessed everything to me.

- Everything?

- Yes, everything, the winter break, the way he forced you to participate in his recreational afternoons as he calls them, your success with Mary and you. No, he spared me nothing.

- And you were okay with that?

- You seemed happy...

Happy? Was he? Suddenly he realizes that in all the encounters, the multiple embraces, he was looking for the pleasure he had felt with Jean-Paul and Désiré. And the moment he finds it again, patatras! Everything collapses. Bernard sends Ahmed away, forbidding him to attend her parties. How will he find him now? And what's more, he learns that his mother and aunt are also taking part in the orgies planned by the director! No! It's over for her, they will do without her services.

- I don't want to go anymore, Mom, I don't want to go anymore... she sobs.

- There, there, calm down. You will do as you wish. I will not force you to do anything, one way or another.

Eleonora presses her face against her mother's chest. It is soft, it is tender. Beatrice pushes away the hand that was resting on one breast. The young girl's eyes are pleading, her lips half open for a kiss.

- No my dear," smiled her mother, "no. Not between us. Not between us... Do you understand?

Eleonora sighed.

- Get dressed. I'll take you to the stores, it will help you not to think about things....